Growing
with
Jesus

To _____

From _____

Date _____

Growing with Jesus

100 Devotions

By Andy Holmes

Tommy NELSON

A Division of Thomas Nelson Publishers

NASHVILLE   DALLAS   MEXICO CITY   RIO DE JANEIRO

Text copyright © 2000, 2014 by Andy Holmes

Illustrations © 2014 by Thomas Nelson

Illustrations by Holli Conger

Published in Nashville, Tennessee, by Tommy Nelson. Tommy Nelson is a registered trademark of Thomas Nelson.

Cover design by Katie Jennings

Thomas Nelson titles may be purchased in bulk for educational, business, fund-raising, or sales promotional use. For information, please e-mail SpecialMarkets@ThomasNelson.com.

ISBN 978-1-4003-2407-1

Library of Congress Cataloging-in-Publication Data

Holmes, Andy.
  Growing with Jesus : 100 daily devotions / written by Andy Holmes.
    pages cm
  Includes bibliographical references and index.
  ISBN 978-1-4003-2407-1 (hardcover : alk. paper) 1. Christian children--Prayers and devotions. I. Title.
  BV4870.H65 2014
  242'.62--dc23
                                    2013042275

Printed in China
14 15 16 17 TIMS 9 8 7 6 5 4 3 2 1

Mfr: Tims / Shenzhen / Feb. 2014 / PPO9286388

For my mother, Martha Holmes, who still cries
when she thinks about how much Jesus loves her.
Thank you for teaching me about that too.

Contents

Acknowledgments

This is the third—and by far the most creative, beautiful, and exciting—presentation of *Growing with Jesus*, and I'm so deeply thankful to you, the reader, for allowing me this tiny place in your child's growing faith. I can think of no higher honor.

I also want to thank the many fine folks at Tommy Nelson for believing in this book—both initially, way back in the 1900s (1999, to be exact) and in this new super fun, super imaginative version. I want to thank a few by name: Laura Minchew, Beverly Phillips, Karen Phillips, June Ford, and a very special thank you to MacKenzie Howard and Michelle Burke who believed it was worth this delightful makeover! I'm so thankful!

Special thanks to my sister, Libby Poor, and to Sheila Ninowski, Peggy Langford, and John Taylor for lending a much appreciated hand to this book. And to Sandy Noe for being such a great example. Always.

Thanks also to my family: Wendy, I love you dearly.

Our son Shelton and his lovely bride, Abby. Our son Robert Andrew; and our precious daughter, Avy, who was still in Wendy's tummy when this book originally came out. Has it really been fourteen years?

Thank you for living lives that inspire me to grow with Jesus.

Introduction

By the time you finish this book, you may have:

- grown an inch taller,
- survived two or more haircuts,
- outgrown your shoes,
- increased your pants size,
- clipped your fingernails six times,
- completely replaced the outer layer of your skin (four times!), and
- worn out 120,000,000 of your body's cells (and automatically replaced them with brand-new ones)!

You will also have grown in invisible ways. That's right—on the inside. How do I know? Because God designed you that way.

The act of growing is very important to God. You can see it in almost everything He made.

Animals grow. Fish grow. Plants grow.

Like you, most things begin very, very small. Look at you now!

You can run.
You can jump.
You can climb.
You can read.
You can draw.
You can imagine.

And by the time you finish this book, you should be able to do these things even better! Why do I say *should*? Because that is partly up to you.

No, you can't make your hair stop growing or force your body to stay the same size, but you can slow things down on the *inside*. How? By making wrong choices.

Will you choose to grow on the *inside*? If so, you'll love this book. It will help you grow up God's way from the *inside* out. Along the way you will also learn a brainload of fun, weird, and fascinating things about your amazing body and about the amazing world we live in.

Are you ready? Then turn the next page!

You're God's Special Project

You [God] made my whole being. You formed me in my mother's body. I praise you because you made me in an amazing and wonderful way.

PSALM 139:13–14

Thoughts to Grow On

Have you ever made something you really liked? A drawing, an invention, or a special project? You probably kept it in a place where everyone could see it and where it would be safe. Can you remember how pleased you felt?

Guess what? God feels the same way about you—only a zillion times stronger! He knows that no two of His children are alike. God is happy with you. God not only loves you; He *likes* you. God is proud of you and wants to present you to the whole world.

★**TODAY**★ Look in your mirror and say, "Hello, child of the King!" Say it five times, and believe it because you are a child of the King.

My Amazing World

Your fingerprints are unlike anyone else's fingerprints. The FBI has collected more than 170 million fingerprints and has *never* found two that are alike.

15

On Butterfly Wings

If anyone belongs to Christ, then he is made new. The old things have gone; everything is made new!

2 CORINTHIANS 5:17

Thoughts to Grow On

Have you ever seen a caterpillar spin itself into a cocoon? An amazing thing is quietly happening inside that silky womb: the caterpillar is being transformed into a butterfly.

God is working an even more amazing transformation in you! And you don't have to curl up inside a cocoon to experience it. God is transforming the "regular you" into the "new creation you." That "new creation you" can do something the "regular you" could never do—it can be like Jesus!

★**TODAY**★ Draw or find a picture of a butterfly. Let it remind you of the wonderful changes God is working in you.

My Amazing World

There are several thousand species (different kinds) of butterfly. Some species of butterfly grow in the pupa (or cocoon) for several months while other species make their transformation into a butterfly within a few days.

A Farmer's Life

Do not be fooled: You cannot cheat God.
A person harvests only what he plants.

GALATIANS 6:7

Thoughts to Grow On

Have you ever heard of a farmer planting corn seed to grow tomatoes? Of course not. Things simply do not work that way. If you want to harvest tomatoes, you'd better plant *tomato* seeds.

The same is true with your life. If you want your life to be truly good, plant the seeds of godly words, godly thoughts, and godly actions in your heart and mind.

★**TODAY**★ **Imagine yourself as a farmer. Think of your mind as your field. What kind of seeds are you going to plant?**

My Amazing World

A giant sequoia tree in California is the biggest living thing in the world. It is almost three thousand years old, 275 feet high, and seventy-nine feet wide! Picture it this way: that's as tall as a second Statue of Liberty standing on the shoulders of the real Statue of Liberty, and is almost as wide as three city buses parked bumper to bumper!

Thank You! Thank You! Thank You!

Give thanks whatever happens.

1 THESSALONIANS 5:18

Thoughts to Grow On

I'm sure you can easily cheer, "Thank You, God!" when fun and exciting things come your way. But what do you do during the hard times? How do you act during the bad times?

Do you groan?

Do you complain?

Do you whine or throw a fit?

Jesus has a better way. Be thankful. If you'll let Him, Jesus will help you find something to be thankful for in every situation—even in your worst times.

★**TODAY**★ No matter what happens, say, "Thank You, God!"

My Amazing World

International studies have shown that people all over the world make the same facial expressions to express basic emotions such as anger, fear, sadness, and joy. So remember: your face often "tells it all."

Jonah's Fish and Tips

"So love your enemies.
Do good to them."

LUKE 6:35

Thoughts to Grow On

Do you remember the story of Jonah? He's the guy who was swallowed by the fish. Do you know that Jonah's biggest problem wasn't the gigantic fish? It was his heart. Jonah didn't want to share God's love with people he didn't like because he knew that if he did, God would forgive them and they wouldn't be destroyed.

God taught Jonah how to love his enemies.

Have you ever wanted bad things to happen to someone you didn't like? Take a tip from what God taught Jonah: always remember that God loves everyone.

★**TODAY**★ Do something kind for someone you don't like.

My Amazing World

Sharks' teeth grow in rows in their gums. Behind the front row of teeth is a second row of teeth. When the front teeth wear out, they are immediately replaced by a brand-new second row of teeth. A tiger shark can go through as many as twenty-four thousand teeth in ten years.

Complaint
Department Closed

Do everything without
complaining or arguing.

PHILIPPIANS 2:14

Thoughts to Grow On

Let's do an experiment.

Step 1

Scrunch your eyebrows downward.
Turn your lips downward. Tighten
your arms across your chest.
Sigh heavily. Grumble, "It's too
hard!" five times.

Step 2

Relax your face. Raise your eyebrows.
Smile. Shout, "I can do it!" five times.

Did you feel the difference? It takes far more energy
to be negative than it does to be positive. That's why
being a grump is so exhausting!

★**TODAY**★ Greet every chore, challenge, duty, and task
with a positive attitude.

My Amazing World

It has been estimated that it takes seventy-two
muscles to frown and only fifteen muscles to smile.

Above and Beyond

"Those [people] who give mercy to others
are happy. Mercy will be given to them."

MATTHEW 5:7

Thoughts to Grow On

- -

Imagine you've made a horrible mistake. However, when you tell your folks about it, they say, "That's okay. We'll give you another chance."

Imagine how relieved you would feel. It would seem as if the weight of the whole world had been taken off your shoulders. You deserved to be punished but were given mercy instead.

★**TODAY**★ Listen. Jesus is talking to you today. He's telling you to show the same mercy to those who have wronged you. Does anyone come to mind? How could you show that person mercy?

My Amazing World

On August 16, 1996, at Chicago's Brookfield Zoo, a female gorilla named Binti shocked the world when she gently rescued a three-year-old boy who had fallen into the gorilla exhibit. Binti brought the boy to the zookeeper's entrance of her cage where helpers were able to take the child to safety.

Eat It Up

"Blessed are those who hunger and thirst for righteousness, for they shall be filled."

MATTHEW 5:6 NKJV

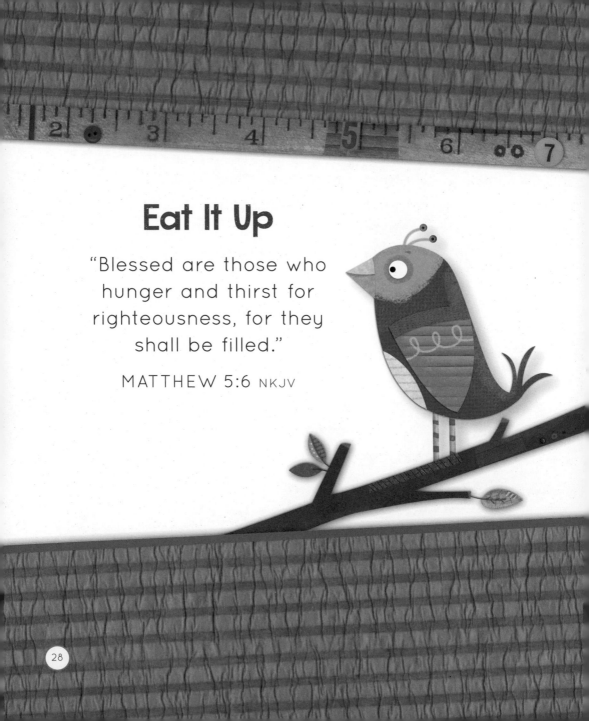

Thoughts to Grow On

Have you ever heard your tummy groan or grumble? That's your body's way of saying, "Hello up there! I need some food!"

Have you ever been so thirsty that your mouth felt as dry as the desert sand? Remember how wonderful it was when you finally found a glass of water and guzzled it down?

God wants you to be hungry for Him. God wants you to thirst for Him. Think of God as food for your spirit and living water for your soul.

★**TODAY**★ Say this prayer aloud:

Dear God, teach me to be hungry for You. Teach me to be thirsty for Your Word. Thank You, Lord.

Amen.

My Amazing World

The human body can go forty-plus days without food, possibly four days without water, but less than four minutes without oxygen (air).

Against the Flow

"Those [people] who are treated badly for doing good are happy. The kingdom of heaven belongs to them."

MATTHEW 5:10

Thoughts to Grow On

Jesus lived His life doing only good things, yet think of how horribly He was treated. He was spit on, laughed at, and beaten. Finally, He was arrested and put to death as a criminal.

What will *you* do when kids make fun of you for doing the right thing? Decide today to stand strong—even if your best friend turns against you.

God will give you the power to make it through these tough times and reward you with His joy.

★ **TODAY** ★ Spy on yourself! Pay close attention to the things you say and do. Make sure you are a leader for good things instead of being a follower of bad things.

My Amazing World

In the wild, horses live in herds (groups) with one horse serving as "chief stallion." The chief stallion is the most fit leader, able to guide and protect the herd.

31

Good-bye, Guilt.
Hello, Happiness!

When our hearts make us
feel guilty, we can still have
peace before God. God is
greater than our hearts, and
he knows everything.

1 JOHN 3:19–20

Thoughts to Grow On

Guilt is that nagging, yucky feeling you get after you've done something wrong. Think of guilt as the rotting scraps in your kitchen garbage pail. If you let them stay in there, they will turn sour and stink. The secret sins you hide in your heart rot and turn sour too. They will rob you of happiness.

Guess what? The only way to no longer feel guilty is to no longer hide the wrong thing you've done. God says, "I love you. Don't be afraid to tell Me about it." And what's more, God knows all about it already. And the best news is that He's not waiting to *scold* you. He's waiting to *hold* you and give you His peace.

★ **TODAY** ★ Tell God about the wrong things you've done. Do it right now.

My Amazing World

The Tasmanian devil is a carnivorous (meat-eating) marsupial (animals with pouches) that eats garbage—and small animals—and is very much in need of a bath. It is possible to smell one miles away.

Remember the Lord

Remember the Lord in
everything you do.
And he will give
you success.

PROVERBS 3:6

Thoughts to Grow On

Imagine you're getting ready to go to school. Think through a checklist of what you'd need to do.

- Get out of bed.
- Get dressed.
- Eat breakfast.
- Brush your teeth and hair.
- Grab your school backpack (and lunch).

Now you're ready. Right? Wait. There's one more thing: tell God, "Good morning," and thank Him for being with you throughout the day.

If you remember God in all that you do, He has promised to give you success. That doesn't mean He'll give you As on your tests when you haven't studied. It means that God will give you strength, wisdom, and courage to successfully handle every minute of your day.

★**TODAY**★ **Remember the Lord in all your activities.**

My Amazing World

A Dall porpoise can go without sleep for three years.

Do Your Best

Whatever work you do,
do your best.

ECCLESIASTES 9:10

Thoughts to Grow On

Get out a pencil and a piece of paper.

Part 1. Hold your pencil firmly. Pay close attention to what you're doing. In your very best handwriting, write: I am doing my best.

Part 2. Hold your pencil very loosely. Gaze into midair and slouch. Once again, write: I am doing my best.

Study the two sentences. Which line turned out better? The first one, of course! Why? Because you truly did your best. In the second one, you did just enough to get by.

God wants you to do your best in everything you try.

★**TODAY**★ Determine to do your best in everything you do. But beware! You'll enjoy the rewards so much you'll never want to do anything halfway again.

My Amazing World

A honeybee makes 154 trips to make just one teaspoonful of honey. In order to gather a pound of honey, a bee flies a distance equal to more than three trips around the world.

God Never Gives Up on You

God began doing a good work in you.
And he will continue it until it is finished
when Jesus Christ comes again.

PHILIPPIANS 1:6

Thoughts to Grow On

Have you ever started something and then given up? Maybe you grew bored with it. Maybe you thought you'd never finish it and you became discouraged. Maybe you really wanted to finish it, but you didn't know how.

God has started a good work in you. He has determined to make you pleasing to Him in every way. He wants to train you to love the way He loves, to forgive the way He forgives, and to do good just as He does good.

So don't worry if you make mistakes along the way (even the same mistakes). God will not give up on you. Ever.

★**TODAY**★ **Thank God for His promise to always help you in every way.**

My Amazing World

A beautiful pearl begins as a grain of sand. The grain of sand enters the shell of an oyster, mussel, or clam and gets covered (and strengthened) with layer after layer of *nacre* (mother-of-pearl). The process takes at least three years.

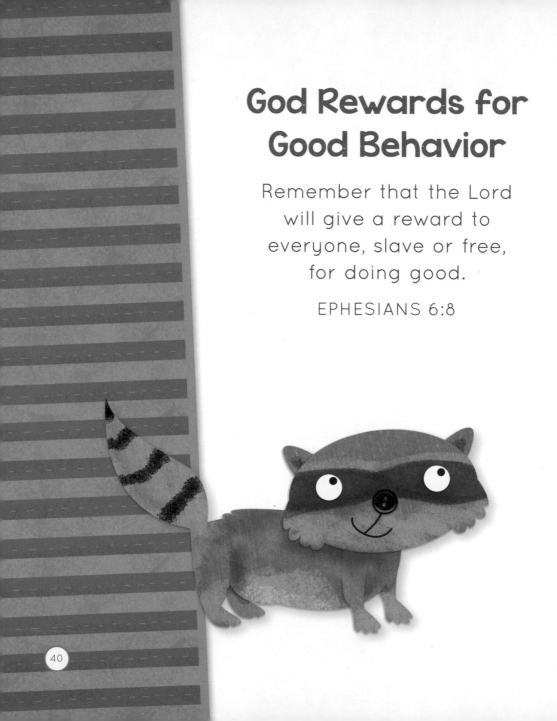

God Rewards for Good Behavior

Remember that the Lord will give a reward to everyone, slave or free, for doing good.

EPHESIANS 6:8

Thoughts to Grow On

Have you ever done a job and been paid for it? Some kids rake leaves, some clean garages, some take care of a vacationing neighbor's pet. But can you imagine being paid for simply being kind? Guess what? The Bible says you will be rewarded.

God has promised to reward everyone for the good things they do. And He'll reward you with something you can never lose through a hole in your pocket. God will reward you with His joy. He will pour His laughter into your heart, and you will grin from ear to ear. Try it out and see for yourself.

★TODAY★ Be a "do-gooder."

My Amazing World

Some bird parents have to bring their nestlings (baby birds) food one thousand times per day.

All Kinds of Prayers

Pray with all kinds of prayers, and
ask for everything you need.

EPHESIANS 6:18

Thoughts to Grow On

Do you cheer when you're bored? Do you whine when you're happy? Do you whistle when you're angry? Or dance when you're feeling blue? No way, right? Why? Because you have lots of different ways to express your many feelings.

Are you ready for a news flash? God wants you to share *all* of your feelings with Him. Pray when you're feeling silly. Pray when you're feeling bored. Pray when you're not really feeling anything in particular. Glad, sad, mad, or, yes, even bad, God *loves* your company.

★**TODAY**★ See how many times you can talk to God today. And remember, whether you whisper or roar, God is always ready to listen.

My Amazing World

When you play a musical instrument, your fingers move to change the sounds the instrument makes. Your voice is like an instrument. Your vocal chords may take as many as 170 different positions to make their own beautiful music!

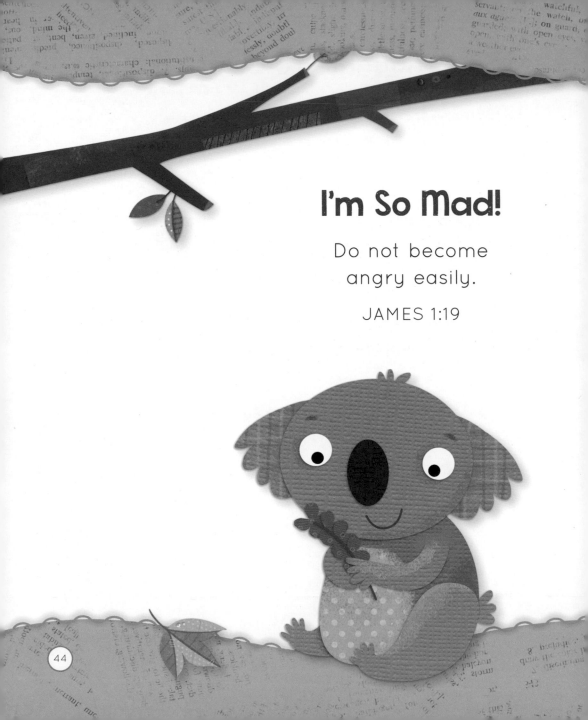

I'm So Mad!

Do not become
angry easily.

JAMES 1:19

Thoughts to Grow On

How often do you get angry? Once a week? Once a day? Once an hour?

It's okay to get mad—even *really* mad. Remember when Jesus chased the money-changers out of the temple? He was very angry. But when you look closely at Jesus' life, you find that He didn't become angry easily.

Do you want to grow with Jesus today? Then determine to be slow to anger. If something gets under your skin, step back. Take a deep breath, count to ten, or leave the room until you calm down enough to think clearly. And talk with kindness about whatever it is that has upset you.

★**TODAY**★ If something gets you mad, use self-control.

My Amazing World

Sloths have a top speed of one mile per hour, making them the slowest of all mammals. Why are they so slow? Their arms and legs are too weak to support their bodies.

Make Peace with Others

Finally, all of you should
live together in peace.

1 PETER 3:8

Thoughts to Grow On

Think of someone you really like to spend time with. No doubt, you both like many of the same things. After all, that's partly why you're such good friends. But do you *always* want to do the same things? Probably not. Is this okay? Absolutely!

So how will you handle those times when you want to do different things? With a smile and an extra dose of generosity. And if it's one of those things you feel like parting ways over, remind yourself how much you love each other, then kindly agree to disagree. If you want to keep the friendship, you have to keep the peace.

★ **TODAY** ★ Determine to be a peacemaker.

My Amazing World

The moon doesn't shine. It has no light of its own. It acts more like a mirror and reflects the sun's light.

47

Do Not Be Jealous

Do not be jealous or speak
evil of others.

1 PETER 2:1

Thoughts to Grow On

How do you feel when you see someone getting something you'd like to have? Does it bother you inside, or are you truly happy for them?

It's easy to become jealous when others get something you want, but jealousy only hurts you. Jealous feelings work like a horrible disease that infects your whole body. Soon, you're full of bitterness from your head to your toes.

The next time you begin to feel jealous, stop yourself. Concentrate on how happy you'd be if it had been you instead of them. Then switch that excitement back over to them.

★**TODAY**★ Decide to be happy when good things happen to someone else.

My Amazing World

In 1439, in an effort to slow down the spread of disease, King Henry VI banned kissing.

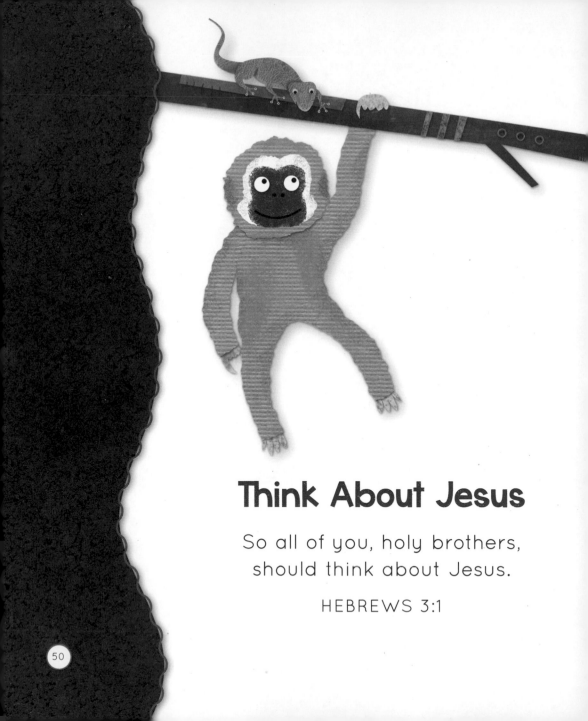

Think About Jesus

So all of you, holy brothers,
should think about Jesus.

HEBREWS 3:1

Thoughts to Grow On

Sometimes it's hard to think about Jesus when you're away from church. After all, you've never really met Him in real life. You don't know what He sounded like. You don't even know what He really looked like.

Yet those are not important things. The important thing is to know Jesus' heart. When you think about Jesus, think about:

1. How *kind* He was. He always looked for the best in people. So can you.
2. How *powerful* He was. He made sick people well and raised Lazarus from the dead! He will help you too.
3. How much He *loves* you. He died a horrible death on the cross so that God and you could be best friends. You can accept His friendship today!

★**TODAY**★ Make this a *happy* thinking day!

My Amazing World

Your brain weighs less than three pounds, is about the size of a grapefruit, and is thousands of times more powerful than the world's most powerful computer.

Be Satisfied

And be satisfied with
what you have.

HEBREWS 13:5

Thoughts to Grow On

Do you remember the story *The Emperor's New Suit*? He was never satisfied and always had to have more clothes. His love for always having the "latest and greatest" fashions soon led him to make a royal fool of himself.

Don't be fooled into loving things. *Use* things. Love *people*. What's in style today will be out of style tomorrow. And that toy or shirt you've been dreaming about will soon break, wear out, or lose its appeal.

Love people instead. Think of ways to show others you care. Be thankful and satisfied with the things you have.

★**TODAY**★ Take one item off your secret I-can't-live-without-it list and never crave it again.

My Amazing World

When you shiver it causes your muscles to move and produce heat. The goose bumps on your skin are caused by tiny muscles that lift your body hairs and cause them to stand straight up. This traps air closer to the skin than usual, which helps you warm up quicker.

Be a Doer

Jesus said, "Those who
hear the teaching of God
and obey it—they are
the ones who are
truly blessed."

LUKE 11:28

Thoughts to Grow On

Imagine you've been given a wonderful gift that came wrapped in an unusual package. In order to get the gift—without ruining it—you would have to follow special directions. Would you ignore the directions and eagerly rip into the package, or would you carefully follow the directions?

God has given you just such a gift. It's called life. Your life has to be "unwrapped" one choice at a time.

If you make a bad choice, you damage this precious gift. Good choices bring blessings. If you make one bad choice after another, you may destroy this gift altogether.

★TODAY★ Make God-pleasing choices today so that you may fully enjoy His gift of life.

My Amazing World

Three babies are born every second around the world. That's 180 babies in the next minute—10,800 in the next hour!

Jesus' Lunch Menu

Jesus said, "My food is to do what the One who sent me wants me to do."

JOHN 4:34

Thoughts to Grow On

Have you ever gone without eating for so long that your stomach growled? Do you remember how good you felt once you ate?

Once Jesus sat beside a well waiting for His disciples to return with lunch. A woman came to draw water. Jesus began talking to her. He told her about God's love. It totally changed her life.

When the disciples returned, they were surprised to hear Jesus tell them He was no longer hungry. "I have food you don't know about," He said. His food was doing God's work.

★**TODAY**★ Let your hunger pains remind you of God today. Thank Him for giving you the living bread: Jesus Christ.

My Amazing World

Every minute five hundred thousand cells of your stomach's lining die and must be replaced. The entire lining is renewed every three days.

Stay Away from Evil

Stay away from the evil
things young people
love to do.

2 TIMOTHY 2:22

Thoughts to Grow On

Have you ever felt pressured by a friend to do something you knew (or felt) was wrong?

It takes a lot of courage to hold out your hands and say no when people you really like are begging you to follow along and do something wrong. And though it may not seem like a big deal to join in, it is a big deal. Why? Because you are going *against your conscience*. That's like slamming a wrecking ball into your heart. The destruction is real, and the wall can only be rebuilt one brick at a time.

Don't let someone else determine your behavior. Make your own choices. You'll be surprised at how powerful you feel when you *think for yourself*.

★**TODAY**★ Will you wear your thinking cap today and make your own choices?

My Amazing World

Your heart pumps about seventy-two times a minute, or forty million times a year!

Don't Say Dirty Words

There must be no evil talk among you. You must not speak foolishly or tell evil jokes. These things are not right for you.

EPHESIANS 5:4

Thoughts to Grow On

Do you remember the first time you heard someone tell a dirty joke or say a dirty word? Deep down, you felt sneaky because you knew you were hearing something that shouldn't be said. Dirty jokes and dirty words may seem harmless, but they're not.

Imagine throwing a handful of mud into a pitcher of water. The mud would ruin the water immediately by contaminating it. The water wouldn't be pure anymore.

Telling dirty jokes or saying dirty words is like throwing mud into your mind—it contaminates it. Instead, God says to use your mouth to say good things that will help those who hear them.

★**TODAY**★ Practice using your mouth to say only good things.

My Amazing World

A grown-up's tongue has nine thousand taste buds. A youth's tongue has more taste buds than an adult's. As people grow older they lose some of their ability to taste.

Have Patience

We also have joy with
our troubles because we
know that these troubles
produce patience.

ROMANS 5:3

Thoughts to Grow On

Patience might sound like something a grown-up needs (and they do!), but you need it too. Why? Because you have to wait for stuff too. And that waiting—when done with calmness and self-control instead of with whining and complaining—is called patience.

Patience makes your life easier and more enjoyable. It keeps you from driving yourself (or others!) crazy while you wait for things you're eager for, such as your birthday or Christmas.

★**TODAY**★ **Start practicing patience. If you find you have to wait around for something, make a choice to do it with calmness and a good, easy-to-get-along-with attitude.**

My Amazing World

The peanut buries its own seeds, which—after a long, slow growing season—produce new peanuts and so guarantee its survival.

Wisdom from God

But if any of you needs wisdom,
you should ask God for it.

JAMES 1:5

Thoughts to Grow On

Wisdom is a word you probably don't use very often. Some people think it means to be smart, but the Bible says, "Wisdom begins with respect for the Lord" (Psalm 111:10).

Without wisdom you will do many foolish things.

"Wisdom will help you be a good person. It will help you do what is right" (Proverbs 2:20).

How do you get wisdom? You ask God for it because that's where it comes from. And you keep on asking God for it. You seek after it as if you were searching for silver. You hunt for it as if you were looking for hidden treasure. Why? Because that's exactly what wisdom is—a treasure.

★**TODAY**★ Begin asking God for wisdom.

My Amazing World

King Solomon's gift of wisdom from God was so great people from all over the world—including the Queen of Sheba—came to hear him speak.

Don't Argue

Stay away from foolish
and stupid arguments.

2 TIMOTHY 2:23

Thoughts to Grow On

"Is not!"

"Is too!"

You've probably said these words yourself. If so, you know that little arguments become big arguments, and soon you're so angry you never want to talk with each other again.

Before arguing, stop and ask yourself: Is this worth fighting over? About 99.9 percent of the time, it isn't worth a fight. Then soften your voice and say, "Let's work this out peacefully. Okay?" Next, you listen. Try to see the other person's side. If that doesn't solve the problem, find someone who can listen to both sides fairly. And ask for God's help. He'll show you how to please Him.

★ **TODAY** ★ Try not to argue at all.

My Amazing World

Talk about getting along! A single colony of ants may have as many as twenty million individuals.

You Have a Special Gift

Christ gave each one of us a special gift. Each one received what Christ wanted to give him.

EPHESIANS 4:7

Thoughts to Grow On

- -

Have you ever been at a friend's birthday party and secretly wished you had been given one of the gifts your friend got? Or have you wished you had a talent or an ability someone else has but you don't?

Guess what? Jesus gave you the gift He wanted you to have. The gifts didn't get mixed up or delivered to the wrong people. Christ has given a special gift to you so that you will use it for Him.

★**TODAY**★ Read 1 Corinthians 12:4-31. It will help you learn about your special gift.

My Amazing World

At least ten million other people have the same birthday as you. If your birthday is in April, May, or June, you share your birthday with even more people.

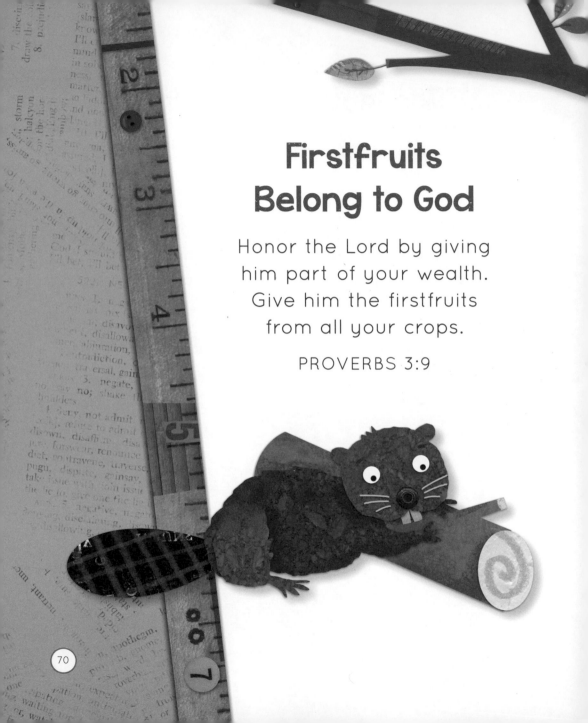

Firstfruits Belong to God

Honor the Lord by giving him part of your wealth. Give him the firstfruits from all your crops.

PROVERBS 3:9

Thoughts to Grow On

This verse is talking about your money. If your allowance is one dollar, give God the first ten cents, twenty cents, or even fifty cents. If you find a five-dollar bill on your way home, give God some money first. If your grandmother gives you twenty dollars on your birthday, first set some aside for God, then enjoy the rest.

You can put God's part of your money in the offering at church, send it to a missionary, or give it to help poor people. The amount you give is up to you. Ask God to give you a generous heart and to help you not to become stingy. Give it happily, because God loves a cheerful giver.

★TODAY★ Practice generosity today.

My Amazing World

The United States Treasury prints 22.5 million "paper notes" in denominations ranging from one-dollar bills to hundred-dollar bills.

Don't Brag

Don't praise yourself. Let someone else do it.

PROVERBS 27:2

Thoughts to Grow On

Have you ever been around a braggart? They may boast, "I'm the fastest runner"; "I have the biggest house on the block"; "The teacher likes me the best"; or, "I'm the tallest person in the school!"

It may seem like braggarts are the happiest people on earth, but they're not. Inside, they don't feel special at all. People who brag are secretly saying, "*Please*, think I'm important. *Please*, think I'm special."

God has made each person in a wonderful way. This includes YOU. Your abilities and talents are gifts from God. Enjoy them, develop them, and thank God for them. Let other people brag about them. And when they do, remember who gave them to you: God.

★ TODAY ★ Brag on someone else.

My Amazing World

Many books list Robert Wadlow of Alton, Illinois, as being the tallest human being in the world. He was born in 1918, and grew to eight feet eleven inches tall. However, the Bible says that Goliath was even taller, measuring in at a whopping nine feet nine inches!

God Works in Everything for Good

We know that in everything
God works for the good of
those who love him.

ROMANS 8:28

Thoughts to Grow On

Life can get hard sometimes. There are periods in every person's life when they feel like their whole world is falling apart. These are frustrating times, and they can make you want to quit trying altogether.

Maybe someone is blaming you for something you didn't do, or maybe you keep getting overlooked in something you're good at. Whatever it is, one thing is sure: God is working in it for your good.

Your heavenly Father knows how many hairs are on your head, and He definitely knows what you're going through. Cling to Him and trust that He will bring you through it.

★**TODAY**★ Give your concerns to God.

My Amazing World

Chicken Little was right. He's the make-believe chicken who, fearing the world was falling apart, went around clucking, "The sky is falling! The sky is falling!" Although there is no reason to worry about it, millions of teeny specks of dust from stars fall to the earth every day, and close to 1,500 larger space rocks fall to the ground each year.

God Listens to Me

I love the Lord
because he listens to
my prayers for help.

PSALM 116:1

Thoughts to Grow On

Think of how special you would feel if an important official or even a king asked you to come and visit with him. It would be a very rare privilege, something that most people would never have an opportunity to do.

An amazing thing has happened! The Creator of the whole world has invited YOU to talk to Him—anytime, day or night. And what's even more amazing, He has promised to *listen*.

Do you have exciting news? God wants to hear about it. Did your best friend move away? Share your feelings with God. No matter what it is, God is right there with His ears (and arms) wide open.

★ **TODAY** ★ Spend one whole minute talking to God.

My Amazing World

Josiah, the "boy king," became king of Judah when he was only eight years old. The author of the book of 2 Kings considered Josiah to be Judah's most outstanding king (2 Kings 23:25).

Don't Speak Evil About Anyone

Speak no evil about anyone.

TITUS 3:2

Thoughts to Grow On

"If you can't say something nice, don't say anything at all." This is a good course to follow, especially when it comes to people.

This doesn't mean to keep silent when people do evil things. (That is a very different situation, and you can often be of great help by speaking up.) Instead, it means that you shouldn't set out to ruin someone's reputation or cause others not to like someone.

Think about it. Would you like it if someone said ugly things about you?

★**TODAY**★ Say only good things about people. Concentrate on their good qualities, and share their good qualities with others.

My Amazing World

While others saw only an uncontrollable, angry, deaf, blind, and mute (one who is not able to speak) little girl, Anne Sullivan saw a young lady who simply needed to learn how to communicate. Anne Sullivan's ability to focus on the good qualities of this little girl completely changed the child's life forever. This little girl grew up to become one of the most admired people who ever lived. The little girl's name? Helen Keller.

Faith Muscles

The Lord searches all
the earth for people who
have given themselves
completely to him. He
wants to make them strong.

2 CHRONICLES 16:9

Thoughts to Grow On

If you exercised for ten minutes every day, your whole body would become stronger. That's how it works with your faith in God too.

God is constantly watching you to see when you obey Him. Each act of obedience to God is like a workout session in faith. God sees your obedience and gives you new power that strengthens your faith, which, in turn, makes it easier to obey again.

But watch out! The opposite is true as well. If you hardly ever obey God, each temptation you have and every spiritual challenge you face will be more difficult to overcome.

★TODAY★ Exercise your faith.

My Amazing World

You use more than two hundred different muscles to walk.

Capture Your Thoughts

We capture every
thought and make it give
up and obey Christ.

2 CORINTHIANS 10:5

Thoughts to Grow On

Can you stop a bad thought from entering your brain? Maybe sometimes, but you can always decide what to do with that thought. God says to capture it. Take it as your prisoner and make it obey God.

When you allow bad thoughts to hang around, you give them the power to destroy you. For example, if you let a jealous thought about someone make its home in your head, you might begin hating that person. Then you'd have two bad thoughts hanging around—and on and on it goes.

God wants you to enjoy life to the fullest. Bad thoughts seek to destroy your enjoyment of life.

★**TODAY**★ **Stand guard over your thoughts.**

My Amazing World

A spider uses sticky webs to catch its prey. Can a spider get caught in its own sticky web? Yes, but it usually doesn't because it weaves nonsticky threads too. As long as the spider remembers how it built the web, it can avoid the sticky threads.

What Do I Wear?

"And don't worry about the
clothes you need for your body."

MATTHEW 6:25

Thoughts to Grow On

Some people secretly fear that no one will like them unless they look like a supermodel. How sad.

God wants you to be smarter than that. He wants you to know that YOU are His masterpiece. He designed you more marvelously than any of His other creations. He made you in His image.

It doesn't matter whether you wear the most expensive clothes in town or garage-sale hand-me-downs—true beauty comes from God, and it is yours already.

★**TODAY**★ If you're a girl, memorize Proverbs 31:30. If you're a boy, memorize Jeremiah 9:23-24.

My Amazing World

Italian painter Leonardo da Vinci's masterpiece the *Mona Lisa* was finished in 1503. Today the painting is so valuable, it is considered priceless.

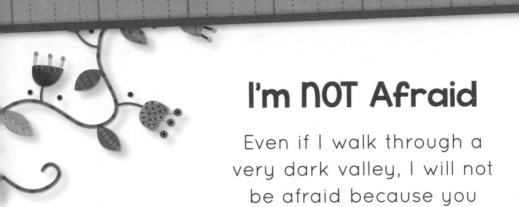

I'm NOT Afraid

Even if I walk through a
very dark valley, I will not
be afraid because you
[God] are with me.

PSALM 23:4

Thoughts to Grow On

Fear has a way of changing things. At night, a shadow turns into a creepy monster, the ticktock of the clock becomes a giant's footsteps, and your heart climbs into your throat. You freeze with fright. Your face turns pale. You feel powerless.

There's only one way out: you must turn fear into faith. How? By reminding yourself of what you already know. Pray a "praise prayer" right then and there—aloud if you'd like. Tell God how much you appreciate His awesome power to protect you from all harm. Thank Him for always being with you (even in the dark). And relax, so that you can think more clearly.

★**TODAY**★ Memorize Psalm 23:4, and recite it when you are scared.

My Amazing World

Goldfish will often turn from gold to white if left in a darkened room.

Say Helpful Things

When you talk, do not say harmful things. But say what people need—words that will help others become stronger.

EPHESIANS 4:29

Thoughts to Grow On

Would you be encouraged if someone called you a dummy because you accidentally poured salt instead of sugar into the mixing bowl? Not likely. Would it help if someone called you butterfingers after you fumbled on the game-winning touchdown? Of course not.

The saying "Sticks and stones may break my bones, but words will never hurt me" isn't true. Words can hurt, but they can also *heal.* Words can break a person down or *build a person up.*

God wants you to use your mouth to *help* others. Before you blab out something foolish, ask yourself: What would help me if it were me instead of them?

★**TODAY**★ Speak positive, helpful things.

My Amazing World

A baby has 270 to 300 bones—more than an adult's 206. The reason? As you grow up, some of your bones grow together. This is called *fusion.*

Control Yourself

You must not be ruled by
the things your sinful self
makes you want to do.

ROMANS 6:12

Thoughts to Grow On

You can change the TV channel with the push of a button. You can lock and unlock car doors the same way. All you need is a remote control.

Some people let themselves be controlled in a similar way by their impulses. They *want* something, so they take it. They *feel* something, so they do it. It's like they've given the devil the remote control to their lives, and all he has to do is aim and click.

Do you allow your feelings, whims, or urges to control you? Or do you think about what God would want you to do?

★ **TODAY** ★ Let God have the remote control of your life.

My Amazing World

Though remote controls seem a recent invention, Zenith developed the first wired remote control in 1950. The first wireless remote control—also created by Zenith—came along five years later. It was called the "flash-matic."

91

Digging a Pit

Whoever digs a deep trap for
others will fall into it himself.
Whoever tries to roll a boulder
over others will be crushed by it.

PROVERBS 26:27

Thoughts to Grow On

Have you ever noticed that every trap Wile E. Coyote sets for the Roadrunner backfires on him?

The book of Esther tells of a real-life Wile E. Coyote named Haman. Haman was determined to get rid of a man named Mordecai, but each evil scheme failed. Finally, Haman built a tall platform to hang Mordecai from. Guess who was hanged from it instead? . . . Haman.

A person may get away with doing evil for a while, but it will eventually destroy him. That's why it is so foolish to try to get even with someone—it will only hurt you more. Instead, simply forgive them.

★ **TODAY** ★ Begin reading the story of Esther.

My Amazing World

The roadrunner is often called the "clown of the desert" because of its funny (or clownish) running style. The roadrunner is the official state bird of New Mexico.

Discernment

"We are allowed to do all things." Yes. But all things are not good for us to do.

1 CORINTHIANS 10:23

Thoughts to Grow On

Do you know you can punch yourself in the nose? It's true, but it hurts! So should you decide to do something simply because you are *able* to do it?

You have many freedoms and abilities. That's why you must develop discernment and self-discipline. *Discernment* means that you can determine whether something is right or wrong, helpful or harmful, wise or foolish. *Self-discipline* means that you can make yourself do the right thing—even when you're tempted to do the wrong thing.

Discernment guides you. Self-discipline protects you. How do you get them? God teaches you as you follow Him.

★**TODAY**★ Use discernment and self-discipline three times today.

My Amazing World

Retired professional football player Herschel Walker exercises great self-discipline when it comes to exercising. He does 2,000 sit-ups and 1,500 push-ups every day.

Honor Your Parents

The command says, "Honor your father and mother." This is the first command that has a promise with it. . . . "Then everything will be well with you, and you will have a long life on the earth."

EPHESIANS 6:2–3

Thoughts to Grow On

Who gives you a place to live? Your parents. Who makes sure you have clothes to wear? Your parents. Who provides you with food, teaches you to make good choices, helps you when you're hurt, and cheers you up when you're sad? Your parents.

Your parents do all these things (and more!) because they love you. God says you should not only obey them—you should *honor* them too.

How do you *honor* them? By treating them as if they were the most important people in the world. By talking in a kind voice with kind words; by obeying their rules even when you're at a friend's house; by being proud of them.

★**TODAY**★ If you haven't started honoring your parents already—start today.

My Amazing World

With seahorses, it's the daddy (male) that gives birth. The mommy (female) seahorse lays as many as two hundred eggs in the male's special pouch. Four weeks later, they're the proud parents of about two hundred tiny baby seahorses.

97

Be an Inspiration!

Let us think about each other
and help each other to show
love and do good deeds.

HEBREWS 10:24

Thoughts to Grow On

It's easier to do good deeds and be excited about serving Jesus when everything is moving along smoothly. But what happens when the road gets bumpy? That's when people get frustrated, or become discouraged and want to throw in the towel.

But YOU can make a difference. YOU can be an inspiration and help turn a discouraged friend around. How? By listening to them—maybe they simply need to know that someone cares. Or you can pray for them, send them a card, or tell them how much they've been an inspiration to you. The main thing is to do something.

★**TODAY**★ Look around. Do you see any friends who need cheering up? Do it!

My Amazing World

Did you know that petting a dog can make you live longer? Studies have shown that petting an animal lowers your blood pressure; relieves loneliness, boredom, and depression; and encourages laughter—the world's greatest medicine of all.

Be Happy-Hearted

A happy heart is like good
medicine. But a broken spirit
drains your strength.

PROVERBS 17:22

Thoughts to Grow On

Do you know that there is a man who was cured of a disease by laughing? Medical experts recently discovered that laughing is a source of healing for the body. When you laugh, your body produces pain-relieving substances called endorphins. These endorphins help fight disease.

Here's more good news: you don't have to wait around until you *feel* happy—you can simply *choose* to be happy. You can make this choice in any situation, at any time. Not only will it improve your health, choosing a happy attitude will make even the least appealing chore a pleasant experience.

★TODAY★ Choose to be happy.

My Amazing World

You can enjoy the sunshine for twenty hours on a typical summer day in Alaska.

You're Not Too Young

You are young, but do not let anyone treat you as if you were not important. Be an example to show the believers how they should live.

1 TIMOTHY 4:12

Thoughts to Grow On

In a lot of ways, it's a "grown-up's world." It may sometimes seem that this makes children less important. But guess what? Jesus told a group of grown-ups to become like children. And the verse above tells you how to turn your world around while you're still young.

Here's how you can be an example for grown-ups to learn from:

- Live for God.
- Honor God with the things you say.
- Share the love of God with others.
- Tell others about Jesus.
- Keep away from evil.

★**TODAY**★ Do these things and you will win the hearts of the grown-ups in your world—and inspire them to do better too.

My Amazing World

Snowflakes—often thought of as tiny—have been recorded to be as big as fifteen inches across and eight inches thick.

Pick Friends Wisely

Do not be fooled: "Bad friends will ruin good habits."

1 CORINTHIANS 15:33

Thoughts to Grow On

Do you choose your friends or do you let your friends choose you? There's a big difference between these two approaches.

If you choose your friends, then you're on the right track. The next question is: How do you choose your friends? Do you choose them out of convenience—just because they live close by? Or do you choose them because you like the same things?

God wants you to enjoy the best of friendships. That's why He tells you to choose your friends wisely. If you don't—or if you let your friends choose you—you may end up headed down the road to ruin.

★**TODAY**★ Think about the friendships in your life.

My Amazing World

There are nearly nine thousand different languages spoken in the world today and one thousand other languages that have been discovered but are no longer used.

Keep Moving Ahead

But there is one thing I always
do: I forget the things that are
past. I try as hard as I can to
reach the goal that is before me.
I keep trying to reach the goal
and get the prize.

PHILIPPIANS 3:13–14

Thoughts to Grow On

Do you remember learning to ride a bike? You had to keep trying until you could maintain your balance *and* pedal *and* steer—all at the same time. You had an exciting goal in mind, and a few bruises and scratches weren't going to keep you from reaching it.

The same is true as you grow with Jesus. You will make mistakes along the way. You will get a "spiritual bruise" or two. That's how growing works. The important thing is to keep your eyes fixed on your goal of growing with Jesus.

★**TODAY**★ Celebrate your victories.

My Amazing World

Bamboo can grow three feet taller in one day.

Overcome
Evil with Good

Do not let evil defeat you. Defeat evil by doing good.

ROMANS 12:21

Thoughts to Grow On

Have you ever stood up for the right thing when others were trying to get you to do the wrong thing? Many times this is all it takes to turn the whole thing around, because good will always defeat evil just as light always overcomes darkness.

Try this sometime: Get a flashlight, and turn off all the lights. Take a moment to notice how dark it is. Then turn on your flashlight.

The beam from the flashlight will overcome the darkness *immediately*. Look closely. You will *never* see the darkness smothering the light. The light is too strong.

★**TODAY**★ Be a light for Jesus today. Take a stand against evil.

My Amazing World
Light travels at 186,000 miles per second.

I Can Do All Things

I can do all things through Christ
because he gives me strength.

PHILIPPIANS 4:13

Thoughts to Grow On

The apostle Paul had a rough life. He was put in prison many times because of his faith in Jesus. He was beaten, whipped, and struck with rods. He was stoned and left for dead. He survived three shipwrecks—once spending two days in the sea—and was bitten by a poisonous snake. He went hungry often and nearly froze during the winters.

Many people would've given up. Paul didn't. Instead, Paul depended on Jesus to give him the strength to make it through any challenge or hardship. God will give you strength too.

★**TODAY**★ Are you going through a tough time today? Lean on God.

My Amazing World

The poison in a black widow spider's bite is fifteen times more deadly than the poison in a rattlesnake's bite.

Be Faithful in the Little Things

"You did well with small things. So I will let you care for much greater things. Come and share my happiness with me."

MATTHEW 25:21

Thoughts to Grow On

Have you ever been given an important job? Maybe your mom asked you to watch your baby sister for a minute, or maybe your dad asked you to help him mend the fence. These types of tasks give you the opportunity to show your parents that you can handle big responsibilities.

When your parents see that you can handle these tasks, they are then able to give you even bigger responsibilities. Learning to be responsible is one of the most important things you'll master on your road to being a grown-up.

★**TODAY**★ Think of something you can do to show your mom or dad that you can handle responsibility.

My Amazing World

Some butterflies can travel as many as six hundred miles without stopping.

Do Your Good Deeds in Secret

"Your giving should be done in secret. Your Father can see what is done in secret, and he will reward you."

MATTHEW 6:4

Thoughts to Grow On

Guess what? God has given you a way to be sneaky and do the right thing at the same time. In fact, He's very much on the lookout to catch you every time you quietly do the right thing. Why? So He can reward you.

Don't do good things like a show-off. Instead, do good things for others secretly. Do good because it pleases God and is truly kind and helpful. And don't worry if nobody thanks you or tells you how great you are. Remember this: God will never forget the good deeds you do—and He sees every one.

★**TODAY**★ Secretly do a good deed for someone.

My Amazing World

The South African wolf spider has a total of eight eyes, allowing it to see in all directions at once.

Be Quick to Listen

My dear brothers, always
be willing to listen.

JAMES 1:19

Thoughts to Grow On

Ask a partner to choose a short book to read aloud to you. (Don't look at the book your partner has chosen.) Now you choose a book to read to your partner. (Don't let your partner see the book you've chosen.) Begin reading aloud to one another—at the same time—on the count of three.

Did you learn much about each other's story?

Now let your partner tell you about his or her story while you listen. Then switch roles, and you tell your partner about your story.

Did you learn much about each other's story this time?

Congratulations! You've just discovered a secret to being able to listen well—close your mouth.

★TODAY★ Be a good listener.

My Amazing World

Neither crickets nor spiders have ears. Instead, they have membranes on their legs that work like sounding boards.

Stand Strong

When a person is tempted
and still continues strong, he
should be happy.

JAMES 1:12

Thoughts to Grow On

Have you ever wanted to do something you knew you shouldn't do? That's called temptation. Some temptations are easy to say no to; other ones seem to never give up until you give in. You're in a spiritual tug-of-war.

Jesus knows all about your struggles. He was tempted too. He will help you be strong if you'll let Him. And when you win, be happy! You will have grown in your faith! What if you fail? God will forgive you and give you power to fight the next time.

★TODAY★ Stand strong against temptation.

My Amazing World

Jim Abbott, a professional baseball pitcher for the Milwaukee Brewers, overcame incredible odds on his way to the big leagues. His fastball has been clocked at 93 mph, he won the 1998 Sullivan Award for being the nation's top athlete, and he has even pitched a no-hitter! Impressive? Here's the clincher— Jim Abbott has only one hand.

You're Awesome!

Say to God, "Your works
are amazing!"

PSALM 66:3

Thoughts to Grow On

Have you ever been complimented for something you did? Maybe you're an artist who amazes all your friends with your incredible drawings. Maybe you're the best speller in class, or the best helper a mom could imagine.

You do these things because you enjoy them. Still, it's wonderful when someone takes notice and says, "You're amazing!"

Guess what? When God hears His children tell Him, "You're amazing, God!" He thinks it's wonderful too.

★**TODAY**★ Take time to brag on God today. Look around and admire His handiwork. Then stare into heaven and shout, "You're amazing, God!"

My Amazing World

Astronomers estimate that there are 100 billion stars in our own galaxy—and that there may be 100 billion galaxies in the universe. Think about it: God knows each star by its name!

Can You Keep a Secret?

A trustworthy person can keep a secret.

PROVERBS 11:13

Thoughts to Grow On

Good secrets should be kept. Here are some ways to determine if it is a good secret. Ask yourself: Is this going to help or bless someone? Is this respecting someone's privacy? Is it something my parents would approve of? Is it something Jesus would approve of?

Here are some ways to determine if it is a bad secret. Ask yourself: Is it something that makes me feel ashamed, dirty, or frightened? Is it something I know I shouldn't be hearing about? Is it an unkind thing about someone else? Is someone's life in danger? Is someone about to be hurt?

★**TODAY**★ **Always keep good secrets. Have no part in keeping bad secrets.**

My Amazing World

The bat uses its hearing—not sight—to find food in the dark. It sends forth as many as two hundred high-pitched "squeaks" per second. The "waves" from these sounds echo off insects back to the bat.

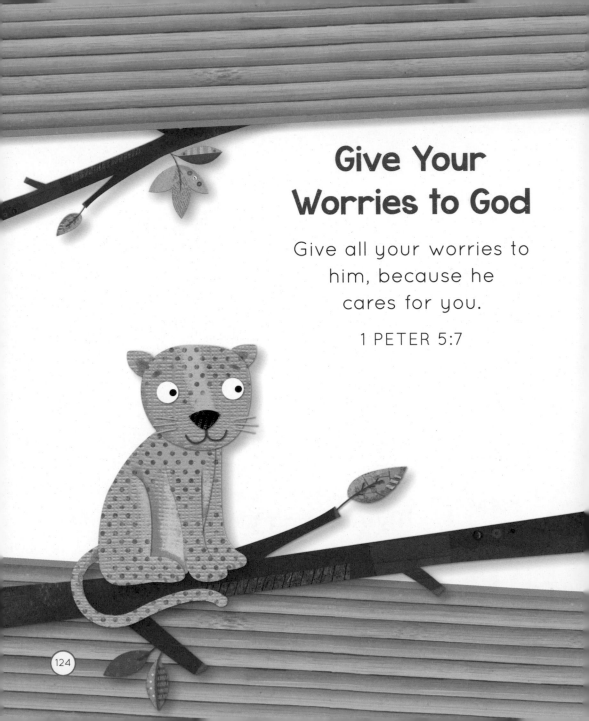

Give Your Worries to God

Give all your worries to
him, because he
cares for you.

1 PETER 5:7

Thoughts to Grow On

Are you worried about anything these days? Do you fear something might not turn out the way you'd like it to? Are you anxious? If so, God has good news for you— He'd like to take those worries off your mind and place them on His shoulders.

You can do this with a simple prayer. Tell God what's on your mind. He has promised to listen and to care. You may want to talk with a Christian friend about things too. Then both of you can pray about it together.

★**TODAY**★ **Worrying wears you down. God wants to lift you up. Tell God what's on your mind today.**

My Amazing World

You grow almost half an inch taller every night but shrink back the next day.

Think Good Thoughts

Brothers, continue to think about the things that are good and worthy of praise. Think about the things that are true and honorable and right and pure and beautiful and respected.

PHILIPPIANS 4:8

Thoughts to Grow On

Did you know that everyone wears glasses? Oh, you can't always see them. These are the glasses through which you see the world, yourself, events, and others.

Some wear *distrusting* glasses. Some wear *bitter* glasses. Others wear *party* glasses—they see life as one big party where they can behave wildly. Others wear *I'm-better-than-everyone-else* glasses (these, by the way, make you blind to all the wonderfully fascinating people you might have gotten to know).

God says, "Wear *love, praise, and purity* glasses." These will help you "see" (experience) things from an attitude of love, praise for God, purity, and truth.

★TODAY★ See for yourself what type of glasses you wear.

My Amazing World

Each of your eyes is made up of around 130 million light-sensitive cells.

Respect Others

Show respect for all people.

1 PETER 2:17

Thoughts to Grow On

The Bible never says you have to like everyone—it says you have to love them. This kind of love isn't something you *feel* (at least, not every time); it's something you *do*—simply because you have made a choice to do it.

This is why you can show respect for someone you don't like. You can treat them with kindness and patience—not because you enjoy hanging out with them, but because they, too, are made in the image of God.

Remember:

- Be considerate of their feelings—even if they aren't considerate of yours.
- Be kind—even if they're mean to you.
- Love them—even if they're hateful to you.

★ **TODAY** ★ Say a prayer for someone you don't like.

My Amazing World

The Department of State of the United States recognizes 195 independent countries in the world. How many can you name?

129

Armor of God

Wear the full armor of God. Wear God's armor so that you can fight against the devil's evil tricks.

EPHESIANS 6:11

Thoughts to Grow On

Clothes are not only for looks, they also have functions. A heavy coat keeps you warm in the winter. A football uniform is padded to keep you from getting hurt (it doesn't always work). A smock helps keep you from getting paint on your clothes.

God has a set of clothes you should wear every day. Actually, it is armor. Why do you need to wear armor? The same reason the knights of long ago wore it—to protect you in battle. And YOU, child of God, are in a battle against the devil.

★**TODAY**★ Read Ephesians 6:10-17. Think about each item of clothing it mentions.

My Amazing World

Your hair may be thought of as part of your body's armor. Hair helps protect your skin from the sun's harsh rays and provides additional insulation from the cold. Eyelashes help keep dust and other harmful particles out of your eyes.

The Spirit Gives Love

But the Spirit gives love.

GALATIANS 5:22

Thoughts to Grow On

Love means having a special feeling of affection for someone or something. You can love your pet. You can love spaghetti. You can love your family. But do you have the same kind of love for your family that you have for spaghetti? No way!

This verse is talking about a special kind of love. It's called *agape* (pronounced ah-gah-pay) love. Agape love is God's love. It is a perfect love He has for every person.

Agape love gives you the power and desire to love even your enemies. God has given you agape love— His own love—as a gift.

★TODAY★ Use agape love.

My Amazing World

Fireflies flash their lights to attract a mate. One type of firefly flashes its light every 5.7 seconds while in flight. Once a male firefly gets within fifteen feet of a female firefly, she will begin flashing back 2.1 seconds after he flashes.

Don't Lie

Do not lie to
each other.

COLOSSIANS 3:9

Thoughts to Grow On

When you lie, you are teaching others not to believe you. You are treating others as fools. It's like you are secretly convinced that they will never be smart enough to "find you out." Worse still, you will have to tell more lies to cover the first lie.

Worst of all, when you lie, you are *destroying yourself* from the inside out. No one can be *truly* happy and be a liar at the same time. It's impossible. You can't be truly happy when you can't respect yourself.

Lying may get you out of something *for the moment*, but it will turn on you in the end.

★TODAY★ Tell the truth.

My Amazing World

You thought Pinocchio had an interesting nose? Check this out: a rhinoceros's horn is made up of lots and lots of hairs that stick together.

The Spirit Gives Gentleness

But the Spirit gives . . . gentleness.

GALATIANS 5:22–23

Thoughts to Grow On

There is a thousand-year-old fable about an argument between the wind and the sun. Each thought it could get a man to take off his coat more quickly than the other.

The wind blew hard against the man, but the man pulled his coat even more tightly around himself. Exasperated, the wind gave up. The sun then heated itself, gently warming the day. Soon, the man took off his coat.

This is a story about gentleness. Often when you try to force someone to do something, they will struggle against doing it. However, if you use gentleness, they will happily agree to do it.

★**TODAY**★ Approach things with gentleness.

My Amazing World

A tornado's winds can reach speeds of almost three hundred miles per hour!

Be Humble

When you do things, do not let selfishness or pride be your guide. Be humble and give more honor to others than to yourselves.

PHILIPPIANS 2:3

Thoughts to Grow On

You've probably heard someone say, "Don't be a sore loser," but have you ever heard, "Don't be a sore *winner*"?

It's thrilling to be the winner, but it is something you should celebrate with a humble attitude. Sore winners brag and gloat. Humble winners are excited to have won, but they don't get a "big head" about it. They know that having a winning attitude is more important than having a winning score.

Being humble means not to think more highly of yourself than you should. God made each person in a marvelously incredible way—and no one is more valuable than another.

★ **TODAY** ★ Choose a humble, helpful attitude.

My Amazing World

In Greek mythology a fable is told of a handsome young man named Narcissus who saw his reflection in a pool of water and immediately fell madly in love with himself. He was so captivated by his own image that he sat and stared at it until he died.

Be Considerate

Do not be interested only in
your own life, but be interested
in the lives of others.

PHILIPPIANS 2:4

Thoughts to Grow On

Here are seven ways to show consideration for others:

1. Say "Thank you" when others help you.
2. Let your guest decide which game to play first.
3. Give the biggest ice cream cone to someone else.
4. Play quietly while someone else is on the phone.
5. Put things back when you've finished using them.
6. Take special care of borrowed things, and return them quickly.
7. Be a good listener.

Being considerate means behaving in ways that show you care about others' feelings. It starts when you choose to pay attention to what others are experiencing, talking about, or going through.

★**TODAY**★ Be considerate of others.

My Amazing World

During a drought, the helmet frog uses its head as the door to its house. This keeps moisture in so it (and the other frogs with it) can live.

141

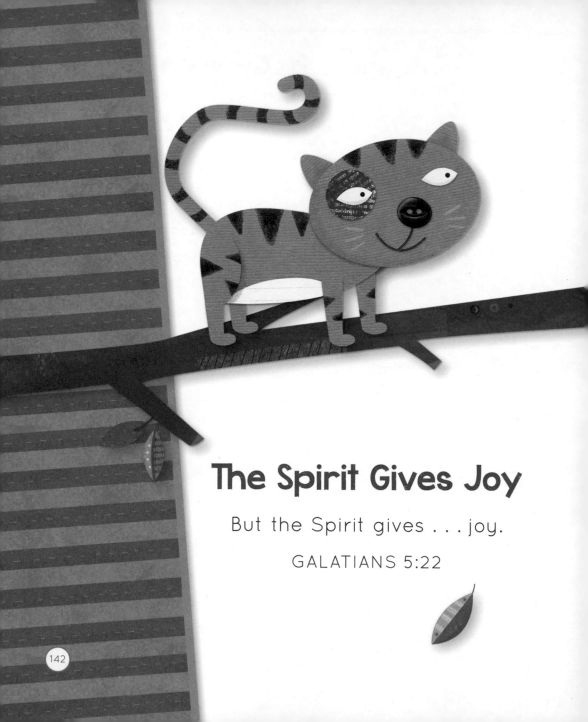

The Spirit Gives Joy

But the Spirit gives . . . joy.

GALATIANS 5:22

Thoughts to Grow On

Think of something that makes you especially happy. Is it a puppy licking your face? Wrestling with your dad? Waking up on Christmas morning? Close your eyes for a minute and capture that memory or experience before you read any further.

Do you still have some of that feeling left even when your eyes are open? That feeling is called joy. Joy goes beyond happiness to delight. Lots of things can make you happy—truly special things give you joy. Today's verse says that God's Holy Spirit gives joy for your delight (Galatians 5:22).

★**TODAY**★ Take a few minutes to think about God's love for you. As you do so, you will experience His joy.

My Amazing World

The laughing hyena can grow to a length of six feet and weigh as much as 180 pounds.

Show Respect to Others

Do not speak angrily to an older man, but talk to him as if he were your father. Treat younger men like brothers. Treat older women like mothers, and younger women like sisters.

1 TIMOTHY 5:1

Thoughts to Grow On

Why did God give you a mouth? Sure, you need it to eat with, but why did He make it *talk*? Did He make it for ugly talk? Did He make it for sassy talk? No, of course not. Then why did God make us able to talk? So that we could understand one another.

How would you feel if someone took your favorite toy or possession and misused it? When you use your mouth to be ugly, sassy, cruel, or destructive, you are misusing one of your most valuable possessions. Instead, use your mouth as a tool in God's hand—to love, to inspire, to encourage, and to bless.

★ **TODAY** ★ Use your mouth for good.

My Amazing World
Flies are able to taste with their feet.

Don't Overstay Your Welcome

Don't go to your neighbor's house too often. Too much of you will make him hate you.

PROVERBS 25:17

Thoughts to Grow On

Have you ever had a friend spend a few days or a week with you? The first day or so was probably a total blast, but by the third or fourth day, you may have started getting on each other's nerves.

Does this mean you don't like each other anymore? Not at all. It simply means you need to spend some time away from each other. That's part of being best friends too.

God made people to enjoy—and *need*—good friendships, but even the best friendships will not fill your spirit fully. You need to spend time alone with God for that.

★ **TODAY** ★ Enjoy your friends today, but enjoy God more.

My Amazing World

Beavers may come home to visit, but they must live at least one mile away after they are a year old.

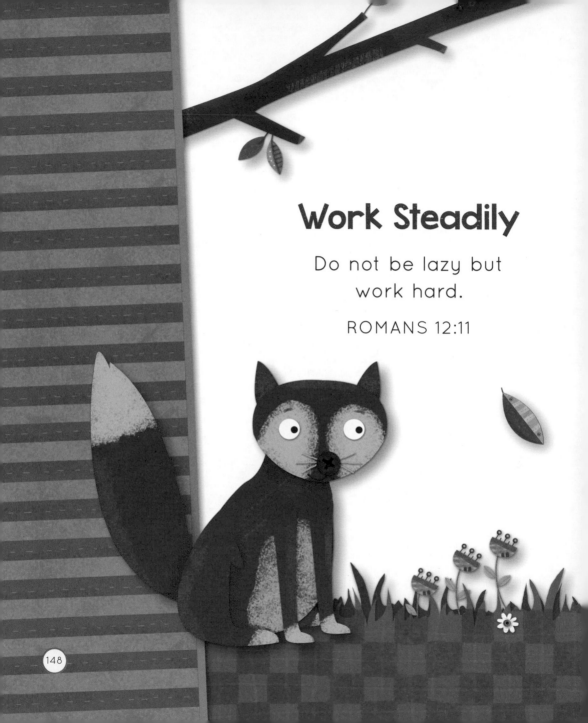

Work Steadily

Do not be lazy but
work hard.

ROMANS 12:11

Thoughts to Grow On

Do you remember the story of the hard-working ant and the lazy grasshopper? The ant worked hard all summer storing up for the winter while the grasshopper played.

You may not need to worry about food for the winter, but you do have work to do. Chores, schoolwork, piano lessons, karate, Bible study—these require work if you're going to do them well. If you do only enough to get by, you won't be much better off than the grasshopper. And even what little you master may be forgotten so quickly, it will be as if you never learned it.

★TODAY★ Work diligently at your tasks. That means to work with focus and great care!

My Amazing World

Pacific salmon travel as many as one thousand miles—often upstream—scaling waterfalls ten feet high on their final journey home.

God Never Sleeps

He who guards you never sleeps.

PSALM 121:3

Thoughts to Grow On

A very insightful four-year-old told his father that God doesn't have a bed. His father asked how he knew this. The child answered, "Because God never sleeps." Oh! What a wonderful truth! You can go to God anytime, day or night, and He is always there!

Are you having a bad morning? Tell God about it. Are things going rough at school? Talk to God! Did your mom make your favorite dish for dinner? Share your joy with Jesus. Did a nightmare wake you up in the middle of the night? Jesus is right there, ready to give you His peace.

★**TODAY**★ Hey, guess what? You can talk to God right now.

My Amazing World

Without enough sleep, your body is more likely to become sick. Sleep allows your body to repair and rebuild and grow.

God Knows Everything

God knows everything
people do, even the things
done in secret.

ECCLESIASTES 12:14

Thoughts to Grow On

Have you ever played the game hide-and-seek? It's a lot of fun, but no matter how good you are at hiding, you can't hide from God. Adam and Eve tried this very thing in the garden but, of course, it didn't work.

God doesn't watch you all the time so that He can write down every bad thing you do.

Instead, He watches over you with the love and care of the good shepherd who eagerly takes care of His sheep (that's *you*). He wants to keep you from harm, lead you beside still waters, and take you into green pastures. Simply put, God wants to give you the best!

★**TODAY**★ **Know that God is with you.**

My Amazing World

Ostriches hide by sitting with their heads and necks stretched out on the ground. Some ostriches have grown as tall as eight feet and have weighed as much as three hundred pounds. Amazingly, ostriches can run faster than horses.

Jesus Comforts You

He has sent me to comfort
all those who are sad.

ISAIAH 61:2

Thoughts to Grow On

Sadness comes when you lose someone or something that you loved. Sadness comes when things don't work out the way you hoped they would—or when you've been hoping for something and it doesn't happen at all.

Jesus is your best friend. He knows what it feels like to be sad. He was sad too when He was here on earth. He knows what it feels like to lose someone you love. He knows what it feels like to be deeply disappointed.

But He also knows the way *out* of sadness, and if you'll let Him, He'll lead you out of yours too.

★TODAY★ Talk to Jesus about your sadness.

My Amazing World

When a person is nervous or upset, the body often releases more acid into the stomach, which, in turn, may cause damage to the stomach lining. Also, when you are unhappy, your heart will usually beat faster.

Do Not Insult Others

Do not do wrong to a person
to pay him back for doing
wrong to you. Or do not insult
someone to pay him back
for insulting you. But ask God
to bless that person. Do this,
because you yourselves were
called to receive a blessing.

1 PETER 3:9

Thoughts to Grow On

Has someone made fun of you? Has anyone ever called you a mean name? Said something ugly about you behind your back?

People made fun of Jesus. They called Him ugly names and treated Him horribly. They shouted one insult after another.

Do you know what Jesus did about it? He blessed them and asked God to forgive them.

When people hurt you with their words, don't yell insults back at them. Do what Jesus did—forgive and bless them. Why? So you'll get a blessing yourself. God will see to that.

★TODAY★ Remember to act as Jesus did when trouble-makers come your way.

My Amazing World

Gorillas usually stick out their tongues when they are angry at you.

Do Not Steal

If a person is stealing,
he must stop stealing.

EPHESIANS 4:28

Thoughts to Grow On

If you've ever had something stolen from you, you know how horrible it feels to be ripped off. You feel angry, invaded, and violated. It can also leave you feeling anxious and wondering if you might be stolen from again. This is a big part of why God says not to steal from others. He knows how devastating it can be to those who have been robbed—even if it's just a little thing that was stolen.

But there are other reasons not to steal:

It's *dishonest*.

It isn't *fair*.

It often *leads to other evil behaviors*.

It *dishonors God*.

★**TODAY**★ If you're tempted to steal today, ask God to help you.

My Amazing World

A cockroach that has been robbed of its head can live for as long as a week without it.

Obey When Nobody Sees

You obeyed God when I was with you. It is even more important that you obey now while I am not with you.

PHILIPPIANS 2:12

Thoughts to Grow On

When you were little, you had to obey your parents whether you wanted to or not. Why? Because they were always watching you to make sure you were safe, and if you misbehaved, they were right there to correct you.

You're older now, and often do activities away from your parents. How are you handling that? Are you obeying and honoring your parents even though they can't see you? If so, you are also honoring God—and yourself! You are showing the world that you truly love your parents, and that you are growing up to be a respectful and trustworthy young person.

★**TODAY**★ Honor your parents while you're away from them (and while you're with them).

My Amazing World

Baby scorpions travel by lying on their mommies' backs until they are two weeks old. Then they can walk all by themselves.

Jesus Is the Son of God

Simon Peter answered, "You are the Christ, the Son of the living God."

MATTHEW 16:16

Thoughts to Grow On

The apostle Peter said something incredible about Jesus. It was something he would never say about any other person who would ever live. He said that his friend Jesus was the long-awaited Savior of the world. He said that his friend, Jesus, was the Son of God Himself.

Can you imagine saying this about one of your friends?

Peter couldn't prove it. It was something he believed. It was a statement of faith, and it totally changed his life.

That was thousands of years ago. Now Jesus is asking you the same question He asked Peter: "Who do you say that I am?"

★ TODAY ★ Will you answer Him today?

My Amazing World

The owl butterfly frightens predators away by the two "owl eyes" designed into its wings. The predator thinks it is seeing an owl and leaves the butterfly alone.

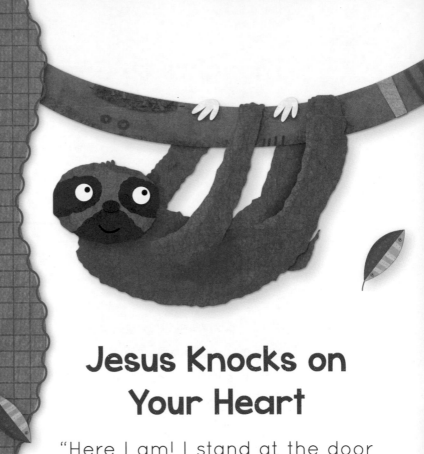

Jesus Knocks on Your Heart

"Here I am! I stand at the door and knock. If anyone hears my voice and opens the door, I will come in and eat with him. And he will eat with me."

REVELATION 3:20

Thoughts to Grow On

The Cat in the Hat is a made-up story about a cat who barges into two children's house while their parents are away. Much to the children's shock (and over the protests of the wise fish), the cat makes a total disaster of the children's house.

Jesus is knocking in real life. He's knocking on the door of your heart. He wouldn't think of barging in. No, He waits for you to invite Him in. And once you do, He will clean every sin in your spiritual house with His love and make everything new.

★**TODAY**★ Will you invite Jesus in today?

My Amazing World

In ancient Egypt cats were considered to be uniquely connected to the false gods the Egyptians worshiped. When an Egyptian's cat died, the owner shaved his (or her) eyebrows off to show how sad he (or she) felt.

Christ Is the Passover Lamb

For Christ, our Passover lamb,
was killed to cleanse us.

1 CORINTHIANS 5:7

Thoughts to Grow On

Do you remember the story of the ten plagues? First, God turned water into blood. Then God covered the land with frogs! The last plague was the worst. God had the death angel fly over the land and kill every firstborn son.

Only one thing would save a firstborn son that night. God told the Israelites to kill a lamb and paint its blood over the doorposts of their homes. When the death angel saw the blood, it let the firstborn son inside that house live. This night is called Passover, because the angel passed over the houses.

Jesus is your Passover lamb. This means that God has passed over your sins because of Jesus' blood.

★**TODAY**★ Praise God for this wonderful miracle.

My Amazing World

A human baby usually spends 280 days (around nine months) growing inside the womb before being born.

Don't Talk Too Much

There is a time to be silent
and a time to speak.

ECCLESIASTES 3:7

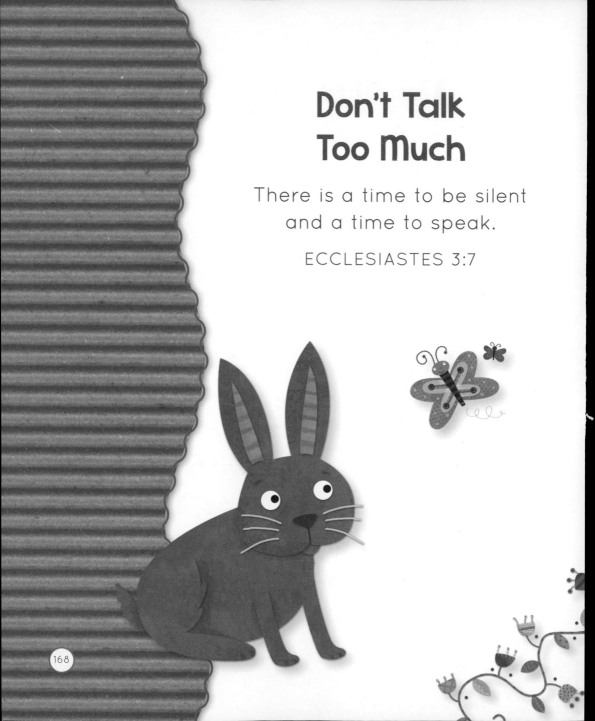

Thoughts to Grow On

You know to be quiet:

- during class at school (unless your teacher calls on you)
- at bedtime (after all the kisses, prayers, and giggles)
- while someone else is talking

Here are some other times worth trying out:

- in the early morning (Listen to the birds!)
- when you're praying (Sometimes you need to listen.)
- when you're beside a stream
- when you don't really have anything to say (In other words, don't talk just to be talking.)
- when someone needs a shoulder to cry on (Be a friend.)

Silence can be a wonderful thing.

★ **TODAY** ★ Try to be quiet more than you talk.

My Amazing World

The German composer Ludwig van Beethoven is considered to be one of the greatest musical composers of all time. Some of his most impressive compositions were written *after* he went completely deaf in 1817.

Peace in God's Family

It is good and pleasant when God's people live together in peace!

PSALM 133:1

Thoughts to Grow On

If you have a brother or sister, you know that sometimes you have conflicts. The question is: What happens next? Do the conflicts lead to pushing, shoving, or calling each other names? Do they lead to bitter feelings?

The Bible gives us two pairs of brothers to learn from: Cain and Abel, and Jacob and Esau.

Cain became jealous of Abel. Cain let his jealousy grow into bitter feelings that led to anger. In the end, he killed Abel.

Jacob tricked Esau out of his blessing. This broke Esau's heart. In the end, they forgave each other and found peace again.

★TODAY★ Strive for peace with your family members.

My Amazing World

Talk about poor family relationships! The black widow spider got its name because the female kills and eats the male after mating.

God Loves Us All the Same

God is not better to princes than other people. He is not better to rich people than poor people. This is because he made them all with his own hands.

JOB 34:19

Thoughts to Grow On

Are you the fastest runner in your school? No? That's okay. God loves you just the same. Are you the smartest kid in your school? No? That's okay too. God loves you just as much as He loves anyone else.

You don't have to be the brightest, the funniest, the tallest, the strongest, the bravest, or the most talented before God will love you. And if you happen to be the brightest, funniest, strongest, bravest, or most talented person in the world, it won't make God love you more.

God loves everyone the same. He has no favorites. There is no competition for God's love—there's plenty for everyone!

★**TODAY**★ Enjoy God's love for you.

My Amazing World

A hummingbird is the only bird that can actually fly backward.

You Are the Light of the World

"You are the light that gives light to the world."

MATTHEW 5:14

Thoughts to Grow On

Imagine you are on a hiking trip with your friends, and you don't make it back to camp before dark. Everyone is nervous and frozen in fear.

Now imagine you could snap your fingers and make a flashlight appear instantly. You'd be the hero of the day! Everyone would follow your every step.

Guess what? That's the way it is in your real world. Without Jesus, people live in spiritual darkness. They can't see where to go. If you love Jesus, you have the light of His power, wisdom, and love to guide others to God.

★**TODAY**★ Let your light shine so that others can see the way to Jesus.

My Amazing World

Our sun gives light to the whole world, and yet it is ninety-three million miles away from the earth.

Inspire Others to Praise God

Lord, let me live so people
will praise you.

PSALM 143:11

Thoughts to Grow On

Have you ever seen a line of dominoes being toppled over one by one? People have set up huge and amazing domino designs where thousands of dominoes bump into one another until all of them have fallen over.

Some call this the "domino effect." It means that a certain *action* will "domino" or "lead to" a certain *result*.

God wants you to use your daily life as a *domino effect* for His glory. God knows that your good behavior will lead to someone else's good behavior. Your obedience to God will "domino" into inspiring someone else to obey and please God.

★TODAY★ Be a "Jesus domino."

My Amazing World

Your body has domino-effect digestion. Take a bite of something, and immediately saliva is squirted on it from under your tongue. Once wet, it can slip down into your stomach. Every day, your body produces about three pints of saliva—enough to fill four soda cans.

The Walking Bible

You yourselves are our letter, written on our hearts. It is known and read by everyone.

2 CORINTHIANS 3:2

Thoughts to Grow On

Have you ever seen someone using sign language? Sign language is a language "spoken" with your hands. People who cannot hear "read" the signer's hands in order to understand what is being communicated.

God wants you to know that your *life* is also a language that people read every day. People watch the way you behave, they listen to the things you say and *how* you say them, and they determine what kind of person you are.

God wants you to be a *walking* Bible. He wants you to live your life obeying His Word so that others will learn how great God is by *reading* YOU.

★ **TODAY** ★ Be a walking Bible.

My Amazing World

Moths do not use their ears to listen. Instead, they hear through hairs on their body.

Be Dependable

You must do whatever you
say you will do.

DEUTERONOMY 23:23

Thoughts to Grow On

Jesus told a story about a man with two sons. He asked each son to help him work. The first son said, "Sorry, Dad, but I can't help you today." The second son quickly agreed to help. "Sure, Dad!" he said. "You can count on me!"

As things turned out, the second son didn't show up. Thankfully, the first son changed his mind and rushed out to help.

How do you feel when someone breaks their word to you? Is it smart to depend on someone who doesn't keep his promises?

★**TODAY**★ If you say you'll do something, be sure and really do it.

My Amazing World

Saint Bernard dogs were used to rescue people on Saint Bernard Pass, a dangerous route through the Swiss Alps. These faithful dogs saved the lives of more than two thousand travelers between the 1700s and the 1900s. One of the last known rescues involved a Saint Bernard finding and waking an almost frozen-to-death boy.

Be a Helper

I know that you
want to help.

2 CORINTHIANS 9:2

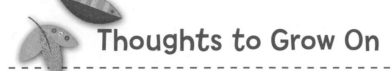

Thoughts to Grow On

The book of Acts tells about a lady named Tabitha. (You may know her as Dorcas.) Tabitha was a very kind woman who loved God with all of her heart. Tabitha was a giver. The Bible says, "She was always doing good and helping the poor" (Acts 9:36).

Sadly, she died, and many cried. Her friends sent for the apostle Peter. As soon as Peter arrived, people began showing him the different coats and shirts Tabitha had made for them while she was alive. Miraculously, God used Peter to bring Tabitha back to life.

Tabitha spent her life doing good things for others. God wants you to do the same.

★ **TODAY** ★ Start doing good things for others.

My Amazing World

A queen honeybee lays up to 1,500 eggs per day. Some queen honeybees lay one million eggs in a lifetime, which means the queen may live only a year or two.

Be a Genius

The Lord's teachings are perfect. . . . They make plain people wise.

PSALM 19:7

Thoughts to Grow On

Would you like to be brilliant without having to be the school's best speller? It's possible!

Would you like to be a genius without having to ace your science test? It's easy to achieve!

Certainly, you should always do your very best to learn all you can in school and in life, but true genius is a gift from God. However, it is a gift God gives to anyone who wants it.

All you need to do is learn and obey God's teachings. But God makes it even easier than that—He gives you the desire to learn His ways and the power to obey them!

★**TODAY**★ Begin your studies as a "God-Scholar."

My Amazing World

Your brain weighs about thirteen ounces when you're a baby, almost three pounds by your seventh birthday, and will be as heavy as it's ever going to be—usually three pounds (the weight of a large grapefruit)—when you're twenty years old.

Be Rich

The Lord's judgments
are true. . . . They are
worth more than gold,
even the purest gold.

PSALM 19:9–10

Thoughts to Grow On

It seems like everybody wants to be rich. You see commercials on TV about it; you hear songs on the radio about it; and every once in a while you may even find a large envelope in your mailbox claiming that becoming rich is as simple as mailing in a reply card.

God has a better way to true riches than any of these. He wants to lead you to the treasure box of riches He has buried in His Word. Each verse you read is a shovelful of the purest gold in the world. God's gold brings you a lifetime of riches, and it can never be stolen or ruined.

★ **TODAY** ★ Start digging for God's treasures.

My Amazing World

A squirrel hides twenty (or more) bushels of food each winter but rarely needs more than two bushels to survive until springtime.

God Forgives as You Forgive

"If you forgive others for the things they do wrong, then your Father in heaven will also forgive you for the things you do wrong. But if you don't forgive the wrongs of others, then your Father in heaven will not forgive the wrong things you do."

MATTHEW 6:14–15

Thoughts to Grow On

Did you know that God's forgiveness actually *stops* when you refuse to forgive others?

Your friendship with God is possible because of His forgiveness. If God were unwilling to forgive your sins, your sins would build an invisible wall between Him and you. But God placed every sin you'd ever have on Jesus and washed them away at the cross. Forgiveness is important because it cost God the life of His very own Son.

Who do you need to forgive today? A friend? A schoolmate? Your mom or dad?

★**TODAY**★ Don't build a wall of bitterness or anger around your heart. Instead, choose to forgive.

My Amazing World

The Great Wall of China is 1,500 miles long, twenty-five feet tall, and twenty-five feet thick. The roadway on top of the wall is wide enough for ten soldiers to walk side by side. It took ten years to build it.

Life Can Be Hard

"But the gate that opens the way to true life is very small. And the road to true life is very hard. Only a few people find that road."

MATTHEW 7:14

Thoughts to Grow On

Jesus says that your life's direction will be determined by two gates: a wide gate and a narrow gate. Although it may not seem like it at times, the wide gate leads to heartache, frustration, and trouble. The small gate leads to true life.

Jesus is warning you to be careful. Do not walk through the wide doors of sin and disobedience even when you see other people doing it. Instead, Jesus says, walk through the small gate. How? By obeying God.

It won't always be easy to do, but it will always lead to true life.

★**TODAY**★ Follow God's path to true life with your choices today.

My Amazing World

It took eighty thousand miles of wire cables and eighty thousand tons of structural steel to build the Golden Gate Bridge.

Be a Servant

So prepare your minds
for service and have
self-control.

1 PETER 1:13

Thoughts to Grow On

- -

Even though Jesus is the Son of God, He lived His life on earth serving others. He once said that He did not come to be served, but to serve (Mark 10:45).

When you choose to serve others instead of trying to get them to do things for you, you're behaving like Jesus. Jesus said, "If one of you wants to become the most important, then he must serve all of you like a slave" (Mark 10:44).

An example is Mother Teresa, who died in 1997. Although she was born into a comfortable lifestyle, she chose to leave that behind and spend her life quietly serving poor people. Many consider her one of the most important people of our time.

★**TODAY**★ Make sure your heart is a "servant's heart." Find a way to do something kind for someone else.

My Amazing World

Your heart is about the size of your fist. It takes about twenty-three seconds for the blood to leave the heart, travel through the body, and come back to the heart again.

God Will Make You Strong

I am sad and tired. Make me strong again as you have promised.

PSALM 119:28

Thoughts to Grow On

Do you ever have days that completely wear you out? It's easy to feel discouraged and irritable on days like these, and to begin treating people badly.

God has an answer for these kinds of days: He'll make you strong. This doesn't mean you'll have huge arm muscles to flex. It means you'll have a new *inner* strength—new energy—to get you through your day.

Here are other things you can do that will help too:

- Get a good rest at night (and nap sometimes).
- Exercise every day.
- Eat healthy food.

★**TODAY**★ Tell God if you feel discouraged or exhausted. Ask Him for His strength.

My Amazing World

An adult kangaroo could jump from home plate to first base in a single leap.

Be a Jesus Volunteer

Then I heard the Lord's voice. He said, "Whom can I send? Who will go for us?" So I said, "Here I am. Send me!"

ISAIAH 6:8

Thoughts to Grow On

Have you ever offered to do something you didn't have to do? If so, you were a volunteer. Do you remember how satisfying it felt to know you were doing a good thing even though no one was telling you to do it?

God is looking for volunteers. God is looking for people who are eager to obey Him. He is looking for people who will do what the Old Testament prophet Isaiah did: stand up and say, "Here I am. Send *me*!"

★**TODAY**★ **When you see an opportunity to serve the Lord today, step up and tell God, "Send me, Lord! Let me be the one to please You in this situation!" Then do the job gladly.**

My Amazing World

Over one million volunteers enable the Red Cross organization to help people all over the world. About four hundred thousand of these volunteers are eighteen years old—or younger.

Be Like Jesus

"I did this as an example for you. So you should do as I have done for you."

JOHN 13:15

Thoughts to Grow On

Can you think of someone you really admire? Often when people admire someone, they may secretly wish to be like that person in many ways. Some do more than wish! They try their hardest to look, dress, talk, walk, and act just like the person they admire.

Jesus wants you to try to copy Him. He wants you to do all you can to talk, act, and think like Him. As you read your Bible, you'll learn what He was really like. You'll discover how He spent His days helping others and how He forgave people when they treated Him unkindly.

★**TODAY**★ Read John 13:3-17 to learn more about Jesus.

My Amazing World

The average child takes nineteen thousand steps per day (give or take a few). This adds up to nearly eight miles!

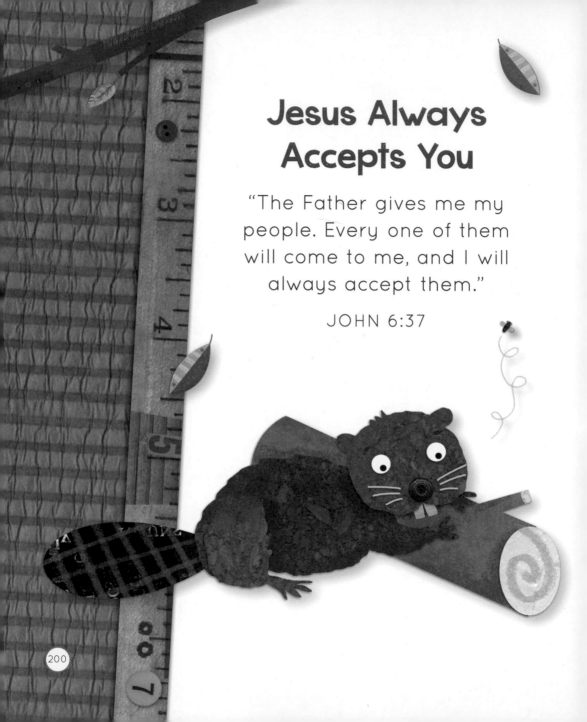

Jesus Always Accepts You

"The Father gives me my people. Every one of them will come to me, and I will always accept them."

JOHN 6:37

Thoughts to Grow On

People can be downright mean sometimes. Some people act like they think you're great one minute and the next minute treat you like a fly at a picnic.

Some people refuse to be friends with someone if that person doesn't wear the *right* clothes, or live in the *right* neighborhood, or go to the *right* school. Sometimes it's for even sillier reasons than these (like not liking the *same* music or the *same* TV shows).

Jesus loves you no matter what and *just the way you are*. He will *never* reject you or be embarrassed to be your friend.

★**TODAY**★ Spend time with your best friend, Jesus.

My Amazing World

Children who live in the rainforest have unique (and practical) clothing styles. The girls wear wraparound skirts and the boys wear loincloths.

Jesus Is Your Shepherd

The Lord takes care
of his people like a
shepherd. He gathers
the people like lambs
in his arms. He carries
them close to him.
He gently leads the
mothers of the lambs.

ISAIAH 40:11

Thoughts to Grow On

When God thinks of you, He thinks of you as kindly and tenderly as you might think of a precious baby lamb. He even describes Himself as our shepherd.

Shepherds are very careful with their sheep. They keep their flock safe from hungry wolves. Jesus keeps us safe from the devil. Shepherds lead their sheep beside calm streams so they can drink. They lead them to the pastures where the grass is the greenest. And if a lamb wanders off, the shepherd leaves the other sheep to find the lost one.

Jesus is your shepherd. He watches over you with great love and care.

★TODAY★ Rest in Jesus' love.

My Amazing World

"Mary Had a Little Lamb" is not only a popular nursery rhyme, in 1877 it became the first words of recorded human speech when Thomas Edison invented the phonograph (record player).

Tell God Your Sins

But if we confess our sins, he will forgive our sins. We can trust God. He does what is right. He will make us clean from all the wrongs we have done.

1 JOHN 1:9

Thoughts to Grow On

Have you ever done something you were ashamed of? You felt yucky inside from your throat to your gut. Worst of all, you couldn't undo it. It was done, and that's that.

You may have felt this about a sin you've done. You feared telling anyone about it—especially God. You imagined that He'd be so mad about it that He'd reject you forever.

Listen. God isn't like that at all. Yes, God hates the bad thing you did, but He loves *you*. He wants you to come to Him and confess—that means tell Him—when you do something wrong. He wants you to admit that you did something wrong so that He can make everything right again.

★TODAY★ Confess your sins to God.

My Amazing World

Soap has been around for more than a thousand years. It was first used by tribes from Germany.

Sing a New Song to God

Sing to the Lord a new song. Sing to the Lord, all the earth.

PSALM 96:1

Thoughts to Grow On

Do you like to sing? Think about some of your favorite songs. How do they make you feel when you sing them?

Some people have noticed they feel happier and more energetic when they sing a song. Even in the cruel days of slavery, the slaves found strength, hope, and power by singing. The apostle Paul and Silas found joy and strength in the midst of their sufferings by singing too.

God wants YOU to make up *new* songs and sing them to Him. These songs will give you power and joy, and will be like a sweet aroma to God.

★**TODAY**★ Sing a new song to God.

My Amazing World

Humpback whales have been recorded "singing." Their songs last from six minutes to as long as thirty minutes! Their songs can be heard underwater for hundreds of miles.

Satan Is a Thief

"A thief comes to steal and kill and destroy."

JOHN 10:10

Thoughts to Grow On

The Bible describes the devil as a "roaring lion looking for someone to eat" (1 Peter 5:8)—something you definitely want to try to avoid. Jesus gives you three clues to determine if something is from the devil.

1. If it will *steal* anything of yours, such as your honesty or your innocence, it is of the devil.
2. If it will *kill* anything of yours, such as your hope or your desire to do good, it is of the devil.
3. If it will *destroy* anything of yours, such as your good reputation or your faith, it is of the devil.

Satan wants to ruin your life. Jesus wants to bless your life. When you choose Jesus' way, you win a great victory over the devil.

★TODAY★ Seek a blessed life in Jesus!

My Amazing World

Not only does a skunk's spray stink, it can make you temporarily blind too.

209

Share

Do not forget to do good to others. And share with them what you have.

HEBREWS 13:16

Thoughts to Grow On

Sometimes sharing feels like giving something up that you were planning to have all for yourself. Everything in you wants to scream, "But it's MINE!" Sometimes sharing means risking that something you love might be lost, used up, or broken. Who'd be excited about doing that?

Aha! There is another side to sharing that actually makes you feel better. This happens when you decide to put someone else's happiness ahead of your own. As strange as it sounds, putting others' happiness first is the surest way to happiness for yourself. God made it so that we would receive by giving.

★**TODAY**★ Share something with someone and see how you feel.

My Amazing World

The "Toys for Tots" program seeks to give every child the simple joy of a new toy for Christmas. It began in 1947, and has collected and given more than one hundred million toys to children.

Jesus Is Coming Back

Men of Galilee, why are you standing here looking into the sky? You saw Jesus taken away from you into heaven. He will come back in the same way you saw him go.

ACTS 1:11

Thoughts to Grow On

How would you feel if you were told that a dear friend you haven't seen in a very long time was coming to your house? Can you imagine how excited you would be?

More than two thousand years ago, Jesus was lifted up into heaven. The apostles watched as He went up into the sky and out of sight.

Here's the great part: He's coming back! Jesus Christ is coming back to this earth someday to share His love with you.

★**TODAY**★ **Look up at the sky today and imagine how exciting it will be to watch Jesus come down from the clouds.**

My Amazing World

The moon is closer to earth than any other space object. How close? Only 240,000 miles away!

My Amazing World

Here are more amazing facts to fascinate your friends!

If you could swim to the bottom of the ocean, you just might see a line of lobsters walking single file (as many as sixty), with each lobster gently holding on to the one in front of it. Call it a "lobster train," if you'd like. Amazingly, these lobster trains can walk as far as ten miles in a single day. Wow!

Picnic attendees beware: the average mosquito has forty-seven teeth. Ouch!

Which is stronger: the strongest man in the world or a honeybee? Answer: The honeybee. Why? The honeybee can lift three hundred times its own weight. In order for a man to do that, he would have to be able to lift fifteen tons!

An ostrich's eye is bigger than its brain.

Bullfrogs close their nostrils and breathe through their skin while under water.

Bald eagles use their nests for many years. Each year they make it stronger by adding twigs and branches. Many bald eagles' nests are as large as twenty feet deep and as wide as nine feet across, and one thirty-four-year-old nest weighed in at more than two tons!

Octopuses and squid have three hearts!

The male giraffe not only has the longest neck of any animal, but it also has the longest tail. Some giraffe tails have grown as long as eight feet!

More Fun Things for You to Do!

In a separate journal, do the following:

- Find and list your own fabulous factoids that will fascinate your friends!
- Write down ten of your favorite Bible verses, and memorize them.
- List your growing experiences! Here's an example:

    Today I disagreed with Jason about the rules of a game.

    I grew because instead of arguing with him, we read the rules together. Sure enough, he was right.

Subject Index

Amazing Facts Index

Scripture Index

Grow in the grace and
knowledge of our Lord
and Savior Jesus Christ.

2 PETER 3:18